W9-BRW-523

SLEDDING

SLEDDING

BY ELIZABETH WINTHROP

ILLUSTRATIONS BY SARAH WILSON

Harper & Row, Publishers

Sledding

Library of Congress Cataloging-in-Publication Data
Winthrop, Elizabeth.
Sledding / by Elizabeth Winthrop ; illustrations by Sarah Wilson.
p. cm.
Summary: Two young sledders bundle into their winter clothes and go down a snowy hill in a wild, whirling ride.
ISBN 0-06-026528-0. — ISBN 0-06-026566-3 (lib. bdg.)
[1. Sleds—Fiction. 2. Stories in rhyme] I. Wilson, Sarah, ill. II. Title.
89-1761
PZ8.3.W727S1 1989
CIP
[E]—dc19
AC

---

1 2 3 4 5 6 7 8 9 10
First Edition

For Nicholas and Eliza,
who know all about snow

The sledding hill's all covered with snow,
time to get dressed and ready to go.

First the tights—
they snatch at the toes,
and pull way up
as far as the nose.

The shirt sleeves are twisted,
the buttons won't go,
but don't give up,
just think of that snow.

The thick red sweater,
all itchy inside—
the arms are too long,
the shoulders too wide.

That suspender just snapped
and came unclipped,
and the zipper is stuck
and will never get zipped.

The socks are sliding down,
inch by inch,
and now the shoes are beginning to pinch.

But don't stop now,
look outside.
Think how fast the sled will glide!

Pull and push,
don't be slow.

The sledders are set and ready to go!

Bang
and bump

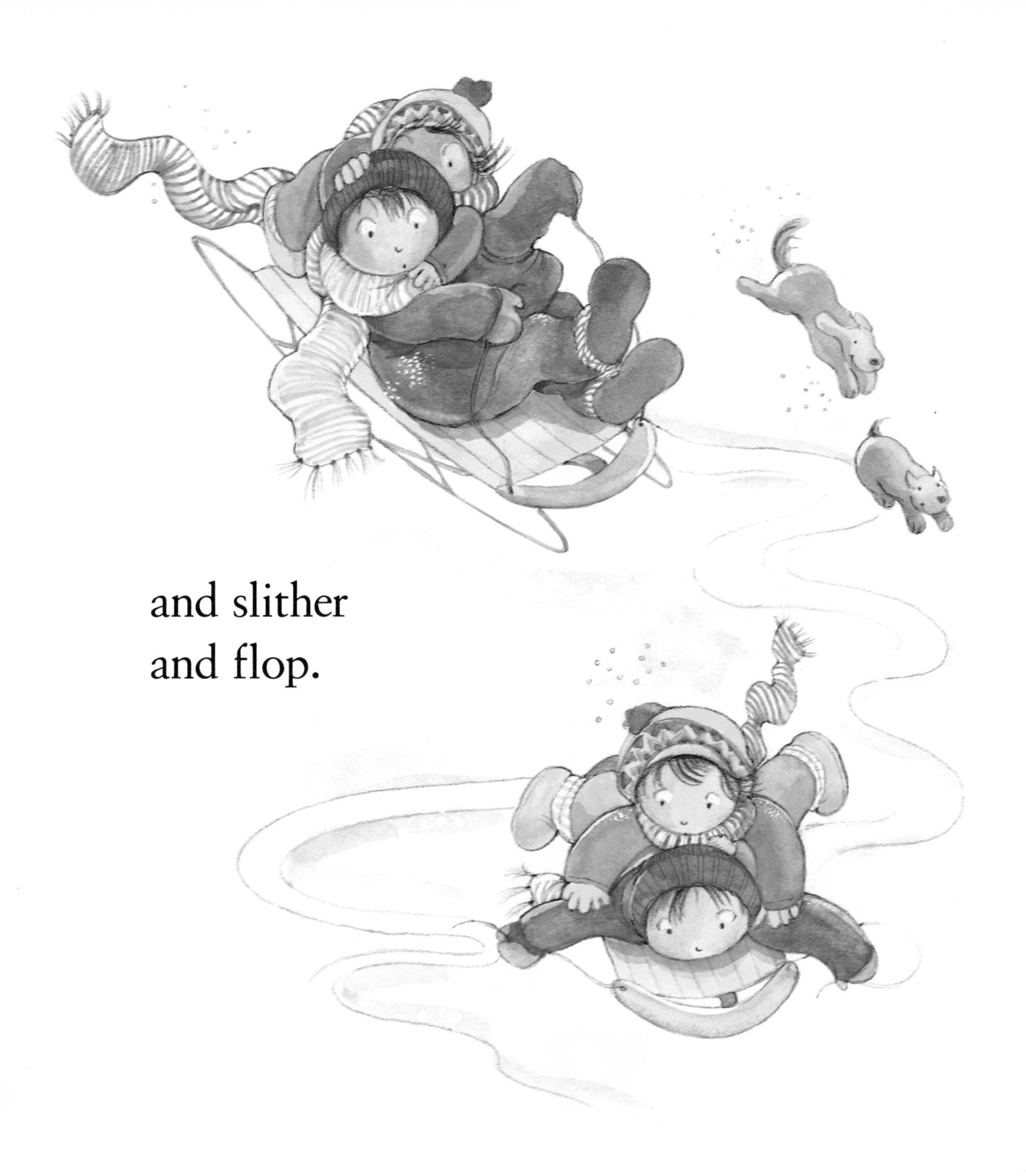

and slither
and flop.

Unzip, unclip, unsnap,

pop!

Hold tight
steer right

splash!

Watch out
don't look

CRASH!

LARGO-KETTERING